THE WITCH'S
CATALOG

by Norman Bridwell

SCHOLASTIC BOOK SERVICES

NEW YORK · TORONTO · LONDON · AUCKLAND · SYDNEY

For Inga and Gretchen

Copyright © 1976 by Norman Bridwell. All rights reserved. Published by Scholastic Book Services, a division of Scholastic Magazines, Inc.

12 11 10 9 8 7 6 5 4 3 2 1   9   6 7 8 9/7 0 1/8

Printed in the U.S.A.

02

If you aren't lucky enough to have a witch living near you, you are missing a lot of fun. For those children who do not have a witch for a friend, this catalog will be a big help. It lists all kinds of witchy things that you can pretend to order for your very own.

Now, for the first time, we bring you this simply super, wildly wonderful, and delightfully dazzling collection of objects, inventions, and goodies, direct from the witch's workshop. You will find here things skillfully selected and cheerfully chosen to bring happiness to every child. Never before have magical things like these been offered at these low prices. Our witchy warehouse is constantly crammed with magical marvels designed to delight boys and girls. Read it and see . . .

SAVE 50%

ON THIS WITCH COSTUME

Look like a real witch. The fine but strong cloth is spun from bat fur and cobwebs. It has hidden pockets for bats, spiders, and crocodiles. Choose any color, so long as it's black. Bats, spiders, and crocodiles not included.

OUR EXCLUSIVE MAGIC FAUCET!

Perfect for thirsty kids. The faucet can be carried with you. Turn the handle and pour any drink you like. Never runs dry. Fill a swimming pool with ginger ale if you like. Of course, the swimming will be sticky.

ORDER SOON!

THE INVISIBLE SUIT

WASHABLE

YOU'LL NEVER SEE ANYTHING LIKE IT!!

Wear our invisible suit. No one will see you. Sneak into the enemy's clubhouse and hear their plans. Walk into the other team's dugout and tie their shoelaces together. Suit box is visible so you can find it when you want it.

A SATISFIED CUSTOMER

BIG BARGAIN MAGIC PENCIL

PRICE IS DOWN SO ARE PILLOWS! MAGIC PILLOWS

Buy this magic witch pencil and your homework problems are over. Just read your books, study your lessons, and the pencil will write out all your homework. Has no eraser because it makes no mistakes.

This pillow is covered with pictures of things you like. The one you rest your head on is the one you will dream about. Choice of ten good things like ice cream, sunny days, friends, puppies, and kittens. Pleasant dreams.

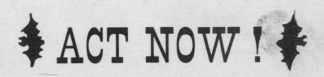

ACT NOW!

LOOK LOVELY IN THIS
MAGIC JUMPER

Here is a magic jumper any girl will love. It's a real jumper. Put it on and start jumping. Be careful — jump outdoors only. Comes only in witch black with bat-bone buttons.

FOOL THE FOLKS!
MAGIC KETTLE

Get this witch's kettle. Hide it under the table. When mom serves icky things like beets or eggplant, just slip them into the kettle and out pops ice cream and cake.

THIS
WITCHY HAMMER

This witchy hammer will help you around the house. Tell it what to do. It will hammer nails without bending them. It will crack nuts and not mash the nutmeats. And it will squash ugly bugs.

HURRAH!
FOR THE
WITCH'S MAGIC SHRINKING POWDER

This is the witch's shrinking powder. Sprinkle it on your dog and take him to school in your pocket. Toss some on bullies and walk on to school with a smile. Shrinking lasts four hours. Handle with care.

AMAZING RECIPES

THE WITCH'S COOKBOOK

Serve your friends some surprises from "The Witch's Cookbook." Make delightful dishes like stewed spider supreme, baked bats with scorpion sauce, roast vulture with toad stuffing, and woolly worm salad. Yum, yum!

SPECIAL!
WITCH'S KITCHEN KIT

While you are in the kitchen whipping up those delicious treats, be sure you are wearing the witch cook outfit. Black chef's hat, black-bat oven mitts, black apron, and witch shoes that carry you around the kitchen at top speed.

THE GOOD WITCH'S SEAL OF APPROVAL

STARTLE YOUR FRIENDS!

WITH THE

MAGIC COOKIE JAR!

The witch's cookie jar is only ten inches tall but holds an endless supply of cookies. Magic cookies don't fill you up. You can eat them all day long and still eat supper. Just twist lid around to change cookie flavors.

A SWEET DEAL!

WITCH CANDIES

Order the selection of witch candy. Enjoy many delicious treats:

Lime-flavored dragon drops
Chocolate brooms
Cotton candy cobwebs
Licorice bats
Sugar-covered spiders
Peanut brittle crocodiles

YUM-YUM

12

EVERY KID'S DREAM

NO MORE BATHS !

Hate washing your hands and taking baths? Don't waste your time. Get the witch's magic bath box. Walk in one side and out the other, and you and your clothes are clean. No more nasty soap.

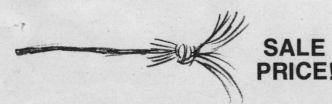

SALE PRICE!

BIG BUILDING BARGAIN!

HANSEL and GRETEL HOUSE KIT

Here is our Hansel and Gretel Witch House Kit. Contains all you need to make a cake and candy house large enough to live in. Includes fudge doormat, chocolate-bar shutters, cookie shingles, candy-cane porch posts, and oven big enough to hold two kids or one witch.

PRICE SLASHED

HAVE THE WITCH-TIME OF YOUR LIFE

THE GOOD TIMES CLOCK!

You should have a witch's good times clock. It makes time go twice as fast when you go to the dentist or wait for dinner. It goes twice as slow when you eat ice cream or go swimming.

THIS MONTH ONLY!

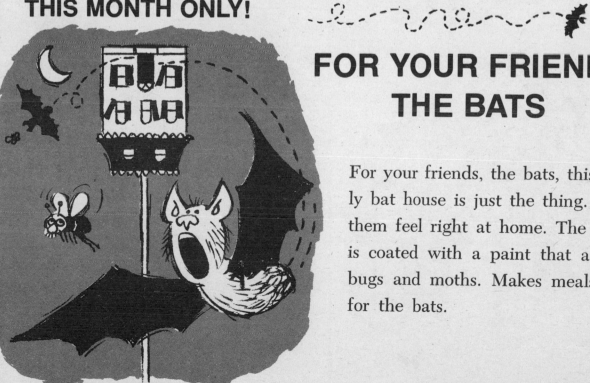

FOR YOUR FRIENDS, THE BATS

For your friends, the bats, this lovely bat house is just the thing. Make them feel right at home. The house is coated with a paint that attracts bugs and moths. Makes meals easy for the bats.

SEW EVERYTHING!!
WITH A MAGIC NEEDLE!

Make perfect witch stitches with this magic needle. The witch's needle will sew beautiful dresses and other things for you. Mends torn pants before mom finds out.

GET A WITCH NIGHT LIGHT

For kids who are afraid of the dark we have the witch night light. Keeps creepy things away. No more bumps in the night. Scary things don't go where the witch tells them not to go.

FOR THE GIRL WHO HAS EVERYTHING!

THIS LOVELY HAUNTED DOLL HOUSE

You will love our haunted doll house. It has five rooms and a spooky attic. Even on bright days the house is dark and gloomy. Has tiny creaking floors and squeaky hinges. Set includes furniture, four scary little ghosts, six small bats, and a frightened family.

WHEN YOU ARE AT BAT

FLY LIKE ONE!!!

For fast footwork when you play ball or race, buy these sneakers. Treated with bat grease, they are as fast as a bat. Put them on and go like a bat. Be careful when you play ball. Rounding second, you might be struck out by the ball you just hit.

PITCH A BATTY BALL

WITH THE WITCH'S BASEBALL!

Be the star of the ball team. A witch baseball makes you the best pitcher in town. Ball has a spell cast on it that makes it impossible to hit. You'll get twenty-seven strike-outs in every game.

ACT NOW! ONLY ONE BALL SOLD IN EACH TOWN!

GIVE THREE CHEERS!

THIS BLACK BOX CAN HELP YOU!

Baffle bullies with the magic invisible shield. When trouble heads your way, press the button on the box and a strong but invisible wall is thrown around you. When they get tired of trying to reach you, just press the button and go on your way.

BIG ENOUGH FOR YOU AND A FRIEND!

GHASTLY GARDENS!

WITH THIS GARDEN KIT!

How about a witchy garden? This kit contains spooky seeds, magic watering can, spidery spade, and dragon-scale rake. Dig a hole, toss in the seed, sprinkle with water, and jump back fast!

TO OWN THIS GAME TABLE!

This card table is great for kids who play games. If your friends can't come to play, just sit at the table. Table plays any game you like. It's a good player, but not TOO good.

FLY THE WITCHY SKIES...
WITH OUR SPECIAL BROOM!

Direct from Salem, this broom can carry three people. It can fly as high as the moon. Look out for airplanes and rockets. It's more fun to fly low so your friends can see you.

NO PILOT LICENSE NEEDED

OR GO, GO ON THE GROUND
ON A NEW WITCHCYCLE!

This spiffy cycle is the fastest bike in town. No motor, no pedals; goes by witch power. Jump on, hold tight, and wish to go someplace. Stops for stoplights and school crossings. Always goes at the speed limit.

SEAT BELT NOT INCLUDED!

A DAZZLING DEVELOPMENT!

AMAZING INVENTION

Send us your picture and your measurements. We will send you this amazing robot painted to look just like you. Dress it in your clothes. Whenever you have to practice the piano or do the dishes, activate your robot and go out to play. Allow six weeks for delivery.

ROBOT CAN LEARN
UP TO FIFTY CHORES

First time at this low price

OUR FANTASTIC MAGIC LAMPS

Try one of the witch's lamps. They come in two models, old and new. Witch lamps have good genies, not mean genies. Rub the old lamp or click the new to get a genie. No limit on wishes.

BATTERIES NOT INCLUDED

UNBELIEVABLE BARGAIN

TIRED OF MOM NAGGING?

Treat your clothes to a witch dip. Mix powder with water and dip your clothes. Then when mom says, "Clean your room. Get your clothes put away," just wave a hand and the clothes clean themselves and jump into closets and drawers.

REAL TV SPECIAL

THAT'S OUR WITCHVISION!

Get a witchvision set. Features the "gimme" button. Press it and anything you like on the screen pops into your room. What you want must be smaller than the witchvision screen.

MEDICAL MIRACLE!

OUR NEW SPOON!

This spoon is well worth the price. When you are sick and mom reaches for some nasty medicine, hand her the magic spoon. The spoon takes the bad taste out of the medicine and makes it taste like your favorite candy.

TOPS ALL OTHERS!

THIS MARVELOUS CAP!

You can escape those weary hours in the barber's chair. When dad says your head looks shaggy, slap on the witch's magic cap and your hair will get short with no fuss or bother. Hair oil not included.

NEVER BEFORE AVAILABLE ON EARTH!
OR ANYPLACE ELSE!

THE WITCH'S WEATHER BALLOON!

Control the weather with this magic weather balloon. Blow it up and have any weather you want under the balloon. Ice skate in July. Swim in January. Or let your balloon float over that picnic you were not invited to.

SLIGHTLY HIGHER WEST OF THE ROCKIES.

(THE PRICE, NOT THE BALLOON)

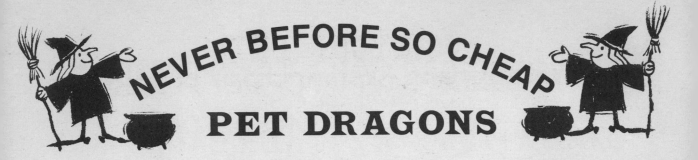

NEVER BEFORE SO CHEAP

PET DRAGONS

Get a pet dragon from the witch's dragon collection. Each is guaranteed to breathe fire and roar loud enough to wake the town. Comes in all colors and sizes. Scales and claws are washable and won't shrink.

FOR YOUR PET
AN ASTOUNDING ARRAY OF PET PLEASERS!

DRAGON CAVE

Your dragon will love this dragon house, shaped like a cave. Made of claw- and flame-proof plastic. Easy to clean. Three sizes: big, awfully big, and terribly big.

DRAGON FOOD

Feed your pet dragon the witch's dragon food. It will please the most finicky dragon. Made of coal and brimstone. Shaped like a knight riding a horse.

LEASH AND COLLAR

When you walk your dragon don't risk losing him. Get our new dragon leash and collar. They are made of tough rhinoceros hide and are flameproof.

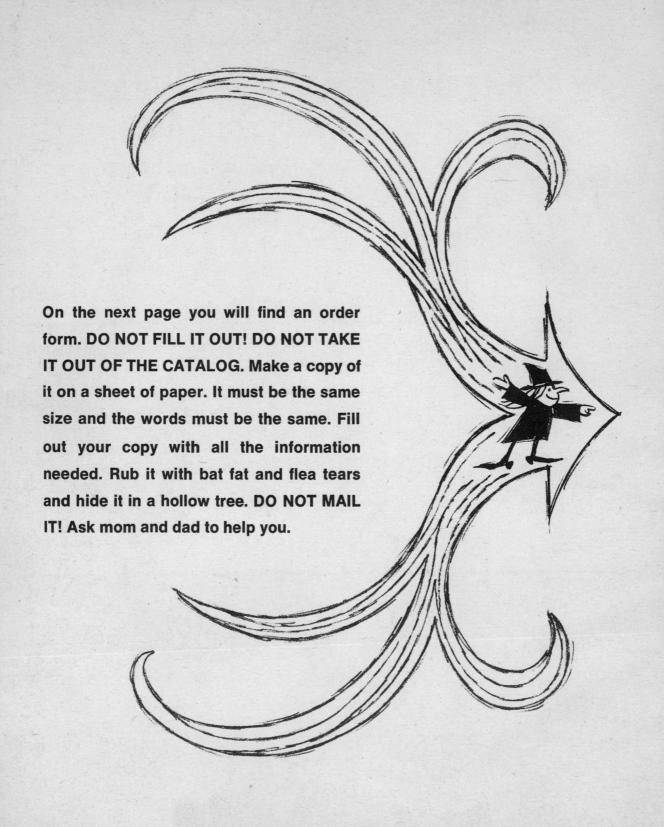

On the next page you will find an order form. DO NOT FILL IT OUT! DO NOT TAKE IT OUT OF THE CATALOG. Make a copy of it on a sheet of paper. It must be the same size and the words must be the same. Fill out your copy with all the information needed. Rub it with bat fat and flea tears and hide it in a hollow tree. DO NOT MAIL IT! Ask mom and dad to help you.

WITCH ORDER FORM

FULL NAME, LAST NAME FIRST · NICK NAME
ADDRESS · STREET · APT NO · BOX NO.
CITY OR TOWN · COUNTY · STATE · ZIP

DO NOT FILL OUT!   DO NOT MAIL!

ITEM	PAGE	HOW MANY?	PRICE	SIZE	COLOR	FLAVOR	WEIGHT

With a crayon make a copy of this order form. Be sure to get all the words in. Then fill it out with all your items you wish to order. Rub it with bat fat and flea tears. Then find a nice hollow tree to hide it in. DO NOT MAIL. SEND NO MONEY.